THE Bedtime Train

Joy Cowley

ART BY Jamison Odone

FRONT STREET
Honesdale, Pennsylvania

Text copyright © 1999 by Highlights for Children, Inc.
Illustrations copyright © 2008 by Jamison Odone
Printed in China
Designed by Helen Robinson
First edition

LIBRARY OF CONGRESS CATALOGING-IN-PUBLICATION DATA
Cowley, Joy.
The bedtime train / Joy Cowley ; art by Jamison Odone.—1st ed.
p. cm.
Summary: As a child falls asleep, the bedtime train rolls
into his room, taking him to a fantastical world of penguins,
a gum machine, and a train engineer named Brad.
ISBN-13: 978-1-59078-493-8 (hardcover: alk. paper)
[1. Bedtime—Fiction. 2. Railroad trains—Fiction.
3. Stories in rhyme.]
I. Odone, Jamison, ill. II. Title.
PZ8.3.C8345Be 2008
[E]—dc22   2007018359

FRONT STREET
An Imprint of Boyds Mills Press, Inc.
815 Church Street
Honesdale, Pennsylvania 18431

For Erica—J.O.

You try to sleep. Your eyelids twitch.

Your ankles itch.

Oh no! You're wide awake again!
We'll have to call the bedtime train!

Can you hear it through the wall?
Hear it coming down the hall?
Steel wheels rumbling on the floor,
rumbling closer to your door?

Now a light comes through the gloom.
The engine's whistle fills the room.
You and the penguins give a cheer.
Look! The bedtime train is here.

The engineer, a man called Brad,
who looks a bit like your own dad,
gives the whistle another blow
and says, "Come on! It's time to go!"

Chugga–chugga, toot-toot.
Chugga–chugga, toot-toot.

Through the gate and down the street,
you smile at everyone you meet.
The people come out of their shops,
and all through town the traffic stops.

The gum machine behind your bed
has a handle by your head.
You pull it and it clanks out loud,
then blows red hearts above the crowd.

Chugga-chugga, toot-toot.
Chugga-chugga, toot-toot.

Into the forest, clickety-clack!
The trees close in behind your back,

and in the darkness, you can hear
a howling wolf, a growling bear.

The penguins flap and shriek with fear.
The wolf and bear are very near.
You pull the handle by your head,
and suddenly the air turns red.

Bright red popcorn can be seen
pouring from the gum machine.
It falls like blossoms on the track.
The wolf and bear both stop to snack.

You tell the penguins, "That takes care
of the howly wolf and growly bear,
but you had better stay awake.
We are nearing Alligator Lake."

Chugga-chugga, toot-toot.
Chugga-chugga, toot-toot.

You're riding high above the lake
when the bridge begins to quake.
Will it crumble? Will it break?
Will you tumble into the lake?

Chugga-chugga, toot-toot.
Chugga-chugga, toot-toot.

You cross the lake but duck because
you're coming to some dinosaurs—
Apatosaurus with long, long necks
and a fierce *Tyrannosaurus rex.*

The penguins huddle in a bunch,
afraid they'll be *T. rex*'s lunch.
T. rex's teeth are sharp and mean,
and you can't reach the gum machine!

Before the fearsome beast can bite,
you're in a tunnel, out of sight.
Into the darkness you all go,
then out again to ice and snow.

Chugga-chugga, toot-toot.
Chugga-chugga, toot-toot.

The train streams over snowy ridges and deep crevasses with icy bridges.

Big white snowflakes fill the sky.
"At last, we're home!" the penguins cry.

The engine stops, and they get out.
They wave to you. "Good-bye," they shout.

You see them waddling out of sight,
black and white and black and white.

Here comes Brad, the engineer.
He says to you, "We're lost, I fear.
Snow's covering the railroad track.
I don't know how to get us back."

"Not a problem, Brad," you say.
"I know how to find a way."
You stand up on your frozen bed
and grab the handle by your head.

The gum machine begins to glow
like a furnace in the snow.
Before you know what it's about,
red gumballs come bouncing out.

The balls line up along the track,
prepared to guide the engine back.
Brad says, "We're on our way again.
You have saved the bedtime train!"

Chugga-chugga, toot-toot.
Chugga-chugga, toot-toot.

You're getting tired, you snuggle down
as the engine chugs through town.

This is your street, and home you go.
You hardly hear the whistle blow.

Your bed is unhooked from the train
and put back in its place again.

The engineer whose name is Brad
now looks exactly like your dad.

He says, "Your bedtime ride is done.
See you in the morning, son."

Chugga–chugga, toot–toot.
Chugga–chugga, toot–toot.